First published in Great Britain in 2009
by Hodder Children's Books

1

A Catalogue record for this book is available
from the British Library

ISBN 978 0 340 98150 4 (HB)
ISBN 978 0 340 98156 6 (PB)

Typeset by
Tony Fleetwood

Printed and bound in Great Britain by
Clays Ltd St Ives plc, Bungay, Suffolk

The paper and board used in this book is a natural recyclable product made
from wood grown in sustainable forests.

Hodder Children's Books
a division of Hachette Children's Books
338 Euston Road, London NW1 3BH
An Hachette UK company
www.hachette.co.uk

CAR-MAD JACK
The Rugged Off-Roader

Written by
JENNY ALEXANDER

Illustrated by
MARK OLIVER

Hodder
Children's
Books

A division of Hachette Children's Books

· CHAPTER 1 ·

Everyone in the Davy family liked
Saturday mornings.

Nico liked going shopping with Mum.
He liked helping her to choose things. He
liked helping her to empty the trolley.

Jack liked going to the Car Supermarket
with Dad. He liked playing in the cars. He
liked making posters for his Wall of Cars.

Amber liked going to her ballet class.
She liked wearing her fluffy pink top and
shiny tights. She wanted to be a ballerina

when she grew up.

But one Saturday morning, there was no ballet class because Miss Marietta was on holiday. Amber was in a bad mood. She pulled the bedclothes up over her head.

'I am NOT getting up!' she said.

'Don't be silly,' Mum told her. 'You can come shopping with Nico and me. It will be fun!'

Amber's muffled voice came from under the bedclothes. 'I am NOT going shopping with Nico and you!'

Mum sighed. 'Well, you can't stay here on your own,' she said.

Amber got grumpily out of bed. She went grumpily downstairs. She ate a grumpy breakfast.

'I'm still not going shopping,' she

grumbled. 'I'll go to the car supermarket with Jack instead.'

Jack nearly choked on his cornflakes. Amber at the car supermarket? Nooooooo!

'All right then,' said Mum. 'It will be nice for Jack to have someone to play with, won't it Jack?'

'As nice as ants on toast,' thought Jack, crossly.

But there was no point trying to stop Amber from doing what she wanted. She always got her own way.

Now Jack was in a bad mood too. He left the table without a word. He grabbed his coat and shoes and went out to wait in the car. It wasn't fair! Just because Amber couldn't go to ballet, she should not be allowed to spoil his favourite morning of the week.

They drove to the car supermarket in silence. Jack stared out of one window. Amber stared out of the other. Nico sat in his toddler-seat in the middle, sucking his thumb.

Dad looked surprised when Amber climbed out of the car as well as Jack. Mum opened her window.

'There's no ballet today and Amber doesn't want to come shopping,' she said. 'So she's going to stay here with you and Jack. It'll only be for an hour or two.'

'Righty-ho,' said Dad.

They stood on the forecourt waving good-bye to Mum and Nico. Then Dad said, 'We've got a lovely Range Rover that has just come in. Want to see it, Jack?' Jack nodded.

'You coming, Amber?' said Dad.

Amber rolled her eyes. Looking at cars was boring, she said. She flapped her copy of *Ballerina Magazine* at them and pushed open the glass doors. She marched across the showroom and flopped down on one of the sofas.

'Phew!' thought Jack. Maybe having Amber at the car supermarket was not going to be too bad. Maybe she would hardly bother him at all.

The Range Rover was parked round the back, outside the workshop. It was black, with silver door handles. Uncle Archie came out, wiping his hands on a greasy cloth.

'Hello, Jack!' he said. He nodded towards the Range Rover. 'It needs checking over and a jolly good clean,' he said. 'You can

help me later, if you like.'

Jack grinned. He loved helping Uncle
Archie. It was almost as good as playing
pretend games in the cars.

They all walked round the Range Rover
together. It was high off the ground, but
there were still mud splashes along the
bottom of the doors. The fancy radiator at
the front had four lights on each side.

There was a green Land Rover badge
on the radiator but the words RANGE

ROVER were written across the front of the bonnet in capital letters.

'How can it be a Land Rover and a Range Rover?' asked Jack.

'Because it's made by Land Rover, and Range Rover is the name of the model,' said Dad.

'Land Rover has been making off-roaders for more than fifty years,' said Uncle Archie. 'They are all as tough as trucks but the Range Rover isn't just tough. It looks more like a luxury car.'

Dad opened the driver's door.

'Look at that,' he said. 'Luxury inside as well!'

Jack said, 'Can I get in?' Dad nodded and smiled.

Jack sat in the driver's seat. He looked at

the dashboard with its buttons and dials and the big satnav screen in the middle. Dad pointed out a big button with pictures round it. There was a flat road, a snowflake, a bumpy track, a sandy desert and a rocky surface.

'You just turn the button and the car adapts to the conditions,' he said. 'The Range Rover can handle any terrain and any weather. It's a very rugged car!'

Jack knew he could have a great game in the rugged Range Rover and he couldn't wait for Dad and Uncle Archie to leave him to it. But they stood around chatting for ages. At last, Dad went back to his office. Then Uncle Archie went back to his workshop and Jack was on his own.

He put his hands on the steering wheel.

What kind of driver would choose a car like this? He shut his eyes and took a deep breath, imagining.

All of a sudden, the passenger door swung open. Jack nearly jumped out of his skin.

Amber climbed in and flung herself down on the passenger seat.

'I'm bored,' she said. 'I want to play with you. Tell me what the game is!'

· CHAPTER 2 ·

Sometimes it could be fun playing with Amber, but most times she was a big bossy-boots. She took over the whole game and spoiled it. Jack wasn't going to let her spoil his best games of the week, in the cars at the car supermarket.

'I'm not playing a game,' he said. 'I'm just sitting here.'

Amber laughed.

'Liar!' she said. 'Tell me what the game is!'

Jack shook his head.

'Honestly, I'm not playing a game. Why don't you go back inside and draw some pictures? You could do some ballerinas. You can borrow my pens if you like.'

Amber crossed her arms. She didn't look as if she was going anywhere. But Jack tried one more time.

'Why don't you go inside and help Mrs Merridew? She'll give you sweets!'

'Dad says Mrs Merridew isn't coming in

until later,' Amber said. 'She's got to look after Maddy this morning.'

Jack groaned. Maddy was Mrs Merridew's granddaughter. She was the same age as Jack, so everyone expected them to play together. But Maddy liked fairies and mermaids and unicorns.

The last time Maddy had come to the car supermarket Jack was playing in a cool camper van. He had his surfboard in the back and he was on his way to the sea. Maddy marched in with her toy fairies and unicorns and turned the camper van into a fairy grotto instead.

'If Mrs Merridew brings Maddy in, I'll have two annoying girls trying to take over,' thought Jack.

Amber was getting cross.

'Come on, Jack. Stop messing around. Tell me what the game is!' she demanded.

Jack thought the quickest way to get rid of her would be to think of a game that was as boring as possible.

'I was pretending I was driving across Dartmoor in the rain,' he said.

'Cool!' said Amber. 'What can I do?'

'You can't really do anything,' he said. 'You're the passenger. You just sit there.'

Amber stuck out her bottom lip. Jack didn't want things to turn nasty.

'Well, I suppose you could read the map. You could point things out,' he said.

He pretended to start up the engine. He checked his mirror. The Range Rover bumped across the grassy moor. Jack bumped up and down in his seat.

Amber looked at him.

'What?' said Jack.

'It's boring being the passenger. I want to drive!' said Amber.

'You can't drive. It's my game,' Jack protested.

'It's our game now,' Amber said. 'And I want to drive.'

She opened her door and jumped out.

She ran round and flung open the driver's
door.

'Come on then,' she said. 'Get out!'

Jack was furious. He yelled at Amber
to go away. She grabbed hold of his arm.
She tried to pull him out of the car. He
gripped the steering wheel with both his

hands. He held on as hard as he could.

'Stop it!' cried Jack. 'You don't even like cars. Leave me alone!'

Amber prised his fingers off the steering wheel and yanked his arm. She was bigger than him. She pulled him out of the car. She jumped up into the driver's seat and shut the door.

'I'm going to tell on you,' said Jack. 'I'm going to tell Uncle Archie.'

'Go on, then,' said Amber. 'He'll only send us both to Dad.'

Jack knew it was true. He knew what Dad would say too. He would say, 'Amber hardly ever comes to the car supermarket, Jack – can't you let her have a turn playing in the cars?'

It was no use trying to stop Amber. She

always got her own way. The only thing Jack could do was leave her in the car and go inside himself. He could make a poster of the Range Rover for his Wall of Cars. But he wasn't ready yet. He hadn't had any adventures in it.

He trudged round to the passenger's side and got in. He would just have to wait until Amber got fed up of playing with him.

'Right!' said Amber. She was happy now. 'Look at the map, and point things out.'

Jack looked at the pretend map on his knee. He pointed to the left. He said, in the most boring voice he could manage, 'There's a stream.' He pointed straight ahead. 'There's a narrow bridge.'

Suddenly, he remembered the glossy photo of Dartmoor in Dad's favourite

book, *Great Britain in Pictures*. He
remembered the high dark walls of the
prison in the middle of the moor. He
shuddered, thinking of the small barred
windows, and the dangerous people locked
up inside.

Jack pointed to the right. 'There's
Dartmoor prison,' he said.

'Oh, yes!' said Amber. 'I've seen a
picture of that in Dad's book. It looks
really scary.'

She pretended to start the engine. She
didn't look in the mirror or pretend to
release the hand brake. She didn't know
anything about driving at all.

'We'll go across the grass to the stream,'

she said. 'Here we go! Hold on to your hat!'

She didn't even try to drive properly. She slid her hands round and round the steering wheel. If she had really been driving they would be doing zig-zags all over the place and riding round in circles.

Jack said, 'We're nearly at the stream. You'd better move the button round to the rocky picture. It's a very rocky stream.'

'What button?' said Amber. 'What picture? Oh, I see!' She reached out and turned it round.

Jack was horrified.

'Not really!' he cried. 'We aren't allowed to really move the buttons and switches. It's against the rules!'

The rules were – No feet on seats, no

food or sweets, no horns or buttons or
brakes.

Jack knew that Dad only let him play
out in the cars on his own because he
always obeyed the rules. Dad trusted him.

But Amber just rolled her eyes.

'Don't be such a fuss-pot,' she said.
'Who's going to know?' She started
pressing all the buttons and switches.

'It's not as if anything will work when we haven't got the key,' she said.

Amber pressed the hazard warning light button. The hazard warning lights began to flash. She was so surprised, her mouth fell open. Jack reached across and switched them off again.

'Stop it!' he cried. 'You are going to get us into trouble. Go back inside and leave me alone. Please!'

Amber looked straight ahead. She seemed to be thinking about what to do next. She chewed her bottom lip. Suddenly, she made up her mind.

'No. I'm not going back to the boring old showroom. I'm going to keep on driving my car.'

'But it's my car!' Jack protested. 'I had it

first. You grabbed it off me. You're nothing
but a horrible hijacker!'

· CHAPTER 3 ·

Amber gave Jack a look. He could see that she was getting an idea.

'That's it!' she said, 'That's what our game can be. I'm a hijacker!'

She grinned at Jack. 'It's brilliant!'

Jack looked confused. Amber explained.

'I've escaped from Dartmoor prison, the one in the picture. I'm on the run and the police are after me.'

Jack didn't want to play Amber's game. He didn't want to play with Amber at all.

'Can't you just get out of the car and leave me alone?' he muttered.

Amber grinned and nodded her head.

'That's right. That's just what you would say, because it's your car and I've hijacked it. You've got to try and get me out of the car. But I'm desperate and dangerous, so you'd better watch out!'

Jack thought about it. Maybe the quickest way to get Amber out would be to play along with her. Cops-and-robbers games always ended up with the prisoner being taken back to jail.

'What's your name, then?' he said.

Amber told him, 'I'm called Bev. Big Bev. I love burgers and I'm built like a bus.'

'OK,' said Jack. 'Then I'm Mark. I'm a mechanic. I've just mended the Range

Rover and I was taking it for a test drive.'

The game began. Big Bev looked up at the sky. She ducked.

'Police helicopter!' she said. 'It's a good job they don't know I'm in this car.'

She turned on Mark the mechanic. 'The

only bit of Dartmoor I know is a small cell with bars on the window. You know your way around. Help me find the best way off the moor.'

'What if I don't want to help you?' said Mark.

Big Bev narrowed her eyes. She made a slicing movement across her thick neck with her finger.

'I'm dangerous, remember?' she said.

Mark the mechanic pointed straight ahead.

'Keep going for half a mile. There's a track,' he said.

The prisoner put her foot down. They bump–bump–bumped across the knobbly grass.

Mark the mechanic was thinking hard.

He had to trick Big Bev. He had to get
her out of the car. Then the police in the
helicopter would see her. They would see
her prison suit and know who she was.

Big Bev swerved on to the track. The
Range Rover skidded on the loose stones.

Mark saw a huge pothole up ahead. The Range Rover crunched and bounced out of it. Mark flew up in his seat.

'Oh, no!' he cried. 'You've hit a huge pothole! I'm all right because I've got my seat belt on but you haven't. You've hit your head and now you're out cold!'

'No, I'm not,' said Big Bev.

'Yes, you are.'

'No, I'm not. Which way now?'

Mark sank back in his seat. 'I'll never get rid of this hijacker,' he thought.

'Which way now?' Big Bev said again. 'Don't make me angry.'

Mark decided to try again.

'Go left,' he said. 'We've got to cross that wide river.'

Big Bev steered to the left. She dipped

down towards the river. The water
splashed up.

'Oh no!' cried Mark. 'You've hit a deep
pool. We're sinking. We'll have to get out!'

'No I haven't, and we aren't sinking,
and no one's getting out,' said Big Bev.
'See? We've come out the other side.

Which way now?'

'Through the woods!' cried Mark. 'Look, there's a gap in the trees.'

Big Bev swung the Range Rover to the right. Everything went dark as they plunged into the woods.

'Oh, no!' yelled Mark. 'You've hit a fallen tree! We'll have to get out and move it!'

'Pah!' said the hijacker. 'A fallen tree's no problem for this car. We've driven right over it!'

The trouble was that nothing was a problem for this car. The rugged Range Rover really was the king of the off-roaders. What on earth could Mark the mechanic do to make Big Bev stop and get out?

They came out of the woods and

back on to the moor. The Range Rover
was too good. Mark the mechanic gave in.
He sat back with a sigh.

'What's the point?' he said. 'Nothing I do
will work.'

But Big Bev was getting fed up too.

'It's boring driving across this moor,'
she said.

Mark perked up. 'Have you hit a bog?'

he asked. 'Does the ground feel squishy and soft to you?'

Mark felt the Range Rover slow down. It stopped. It started to sink!

'You're right,' cried Bev. 'We're sinking in a big bog. What can we do now?'

The hostage and the prisoner looked out the windows. They were surrounded by thick deep mud. It was nearly up to the

bottom of the doors.

'We can't go on,' Bev said. She got out and landed with a splosh in the black gooey mud. Mark the mechanic thought of sliding across into the driver's seat, but even with his amazing driving skills he didn't think he could get the Range Rover out of the bog. Besides, Big Bev could always drag him out and take over again.

Mark got out too. He waded through the mud. It was half way up his legs.

'What are we going to do now?' he said.

Big Bev shrugged her shoulders. She shook her head. Then she saw something behind Mark the mechanic that made her gasp.

'They're here!' she whispered. 'How did they find me so quickly?'

Two big officers and a police dog were coming across the moor. Big Bev looked around, wildly. Out here in the middle of the moor, there was nothing. No trees, no tracks, no buildings. Even if she could wade out of the bog quick enough, there was nowhere to hide.

The dog stood barking at the edge of the bog as the officers came wading towards them.

· CHAPTER 4 ·

Dad and Mrs Merridew were coming across the yard. Maddy was running ahead, but when she saw Amber, she stopped. She didn't really know Amber, so she felt shy. She hung back, waiting for Mrs Merridew and Dad to catch up.

Maddy was dressed like a fairy in a frilly skirt and white tights. Dad and Mrs Merridew overtook her and she fluttered along behind them. Jack wished he could jump back up into the Range Rover and lock all the doors. He wished he could really drive out of the car supermarket and go far, far away.

'Hello, Jack,' said Mrs Merridew. 'I see you've got Amber to play with today. You must be really happy!'

'As happy as a fish in a sandpit,' thought Jack. He tried to smile.

'And now you've got Maddy as well,' added Mrs Merridew. 'She was supposed to be at ballet but I forgot there weren't any classes today.'

'That's why I'm in my ballet clothes,' Maddy said, shyly. 'We went, and Miss Marietta wasn't there.'

'I go to Miss Marietta's classes,' Amber said. 'Are you in the beginners?'

Maddy nodded.

'I wish there was a class today,' she said. 'It's much better than coming to the car supermarket.'

Amber had an idea. 'I could be your

ballet teacher if you like,' she said. 'I'm in the top class and I know all the steps.'

'Ooh, yes please!' said Maddy. She did a little twirl on her tiptoes for joy.

'We can have our own ballet class in the showroom,' said Amber. 'You can call me Miss Amberetta!'

The two girls skipped and danced their way back across the yard with Mrs Merridew. Dad looked at Jack.

'It looks like you're all on your own again,' he said. 'Or would you like to join Miss Amberetta's ballet class?'

Jack shook his head. No way!

Dad strolled back inside after the others. Jack looked at the rugged Range Rover. He waited until he was sure they had really gone. Then he climbed back up into the driver's seat. He shut his eyes and took a deep breath.

Jack put his hands on the steering wheel. He was in control again. Amber didn't know how to have adventures in the cars at the car supermarket. She didn't do it properly. She messed around. She broke the rules.

The whole point about car adventures was the driving. You had to imagine how it would feel to really drive the car. You had to use your skills. A car like this Range Rover could take you anywhere. You wouldn't even have to stay on the roads. But you would have to be a good driver – a driver like Jason Mason!

Jack imagined he was the famous TV presenter, Jason Mason, from the top show, *Wonderful Wheels!* He was doing a programme on off-road cars. He had test-driven six already and now he was going to test-drive the Range Rover.

Jason Mason opened the driver's door and looked at the camera. A sound man held a fluffy microphone on a pole just in front of him. Jason gave the viewers a moment to notice how cool he looked in his brown leather jacket before he started talking.

'I've saved the best till last,' he said to the

camera. 'The rugged Range Rover. It's got guts. It's got style.'

Jason Mason grinned at the camera, flashing his super-white teeth. He pointed to the button on the dashboard with the flat road, snowflake, bumpy track, rocky ground and sandy desert pictures.

'They say all you have to do is turn this button and the Range Rover can tackle any road conditions. Let's see if it can tackle our super-tough course!'

The camera pulled away from Jason Mason to take in the road and the countryside beyond. You could see rocky rivers, stony and muddy tracks, miles of lumpy grass and a ridge of wind-swept sand dunes in the distance.

'This is where the army test their tanks,'

said Jason Mason. 'It doesn't come tougher than this!'

He shut the door. He started the car. He held up his hand, with his fingers crossed. Then he revved the engine and he was off!

First, he tested the rugged Range Rover on the road. He turned the button to the flat road picture. He drove fast into the bends and it didn't skid. He drove fast up the hills and the big engine didn't struggle at all.

He slowed down to talk to the in-car camera.

'Well it drives like a dream on the road,' he said. 'But it was made to go off-road, and that's what we're going to do now!'

Jason Mason pulled off the road and on to a stony track. It was full of big potholes. He switched the button to the rocky picture. A normal car would have bashed its bottom on the ground, but the Range Rover rode over the stones and potholes like a big ship riding the waves.

'I think I'm in love!' cried Jason Mason. 'I'm in love with this wonderful car!'

The track ran down towards a wide stream.

Splash! The Range Rover hit the water.

Whoosh! The water rushed around the wheels.

Bump, bump, splosh! The Range Rover

slowly crossed to the other side.

Jason Mason looked at the muddy bank up ahead. There were deep ruts and skid marks. He turned the button to the picture of the rutted track. He gripped the steering wheel.

Lots of cars would not be able to get up the muddy bank. They would slide off to the side, or fall back into the water. But the Range Rover did not let Jason down.

It climbed up to the top of the bank and
dipped easily down on to the track to the
other side.

Almost straight away, the track ran out.
Jason bounced up and down as he drove
across the lumpy grass.

'We're coming up to the final challenge,'
he said in a wobbly voice. 'We've tested this

beast of a car on stony tracks and rocky rivers. We've tested it on muddy slopes and bumpy grass. No problem! But how will it cope with the sand dunes?'

He bumped his way towards the windswept dunes with their tufts of wiry grass. He could just make out a track, but sand had blown across it, so it was hard to see. He switched the button to the sandy desert picture.

'Here we go!' he yelled.

· CHAPTER 5 ·

Jason Mason wasn't just a top TV presenter. He was also an ace driver. He had driven everything from a go-kart to a lorry on *Wonderful Wheels!* He needed all his driving skills now.

Clouds of sand flew up behind him as he drove the Range Rover up on to the dunes. He couldn't see where he was going. He kept swerving off the firm sand of the track on to the softer sand on each side. Sometimes he thought he was going to sink in too deep and have to stop.

It was tough driving, but Jason Mason still managed to talk to the viewers at the same time.

'Of course, you can't normally drive on beaches and dunes,' he said. 'You would do a lot of damage. That's why we had to use this army training ground.'

He flashed a grin at the in-car camera.

'That's the best thing about being on *Wonderful Wheels!* You get to drive in all kinds of places most people can never drive. Plus you get to drive all sorts of cars most people could never afford to buy. I love this job!'

In that split second of not looking where he was going, Jason Mason lost control of the car and swerved away from the track.

He hit a hard grassy ridge. The car tilted over.

'Woooooah!' yelled Jason Mason, as if he was a cowboy riding a massive horse.

By the time he had got control again he had lost his bearings. There was a camera crew waiting for him somewhere at the top – but where? He slowed right down. The

dusty clouds began to settle.

Then Jason Mason saw the glint of sunlight on metal up ahead. He drove towards it. The camera crew cheered as he came into sight. He pulled up in front of them, and flung open the door.

'I have only one word for you, my friends,' he declared. 'That word is — wonderful!'

He gave viewers a moment to admire his famous curly hair and brown leather jacket before going on.

'This Range Rover is as tough as a truck, but it looks like a luxury car even when it's covered in mud and sand.'

The camera moved from Jason Mason to the rugged Range Rover. It lingered on the mud splashes on the doors. It ran slowly across the film of sand on the paintwork and windows. Then the music came on and it was the end of *Wonderful Wheels!*

Jack sighed. He wasn't Jason Mason any more. It had been a great game. Now he was ready to make his poster.

He went into the showroom. Miss Amberetta was teaching Maddie some sort of ballet jump in the space by the back windows. They were a nice long way away from the sofas and the low table where Jack liked to do his drawings.

Jack got out his felt pens and colouring pencils. He opened his drawing pad. He looked at the blank paper for a few minutes, until the picture in his mind was really clear. Then he started to draw.

He had just begun colouring in when

Mum arrived. Nico was asleep in the car.
All that grabbing things off the shelves and
throwing things out of the trolley had worn
him out. Mum looked a bit worn out too.

'Oh!' Jack groaned. 'Do I have to go
home now? It isn't lunchtime yet.'

'No,' said Mum. 'I've just come to pick up
Amber. Dad can bring you home later, as
usual.'

On the upside, thought Jack, that gets
rid of Amber. On the downside, when
Amber had gone home, Maddy would want
someone to play with.

'Can Maddy come back and play at our
house?' Amber asked Mum.

'Yes!' thought Jack. 'Please say yes!'

Mum did say yes, and Mrs Merridew
agreed.

Mum, Nico, Amber and Maddy went off in the car. Jack settled back to his poster. Mrs Merridew brought him some milk and home-made biscuits. Dad saw a customer and went out to talk to him. Everything was back to normal, and Jack was happy.

He finished the picture and wrote underneath:

'Range Rover. It is very rugged. It has a special button for going over rocks and rivers and mud and sand. It is a top car, so watch out that no one tries to pinch it off you!'

Dad brought the customer inside to take down some details. He was wearing a black leather jacket and he looked as if he had plenty of money.

'I'm looking for an off-roader,' he said.

'Not sure what kind, but I'll know it when I see it.'

While Dad was filling in a form, the customer glanced across at Jack. He leaned over to look at Jack's poster.

'Nice car!' he said. 'It's a pity you haven't got something like that in at the moment.'

'But we have,' said Jack. 'It's just not

ready to put in the showroom.
It's still round the back.'

Jack's Dad asked the
customer if he could
come back in the
afternoon. 'We'll have
it ready by then,' he
said. What he meant was,
it would be cleaned and
polished inside and out. It
would look like new. The customer
dithered.

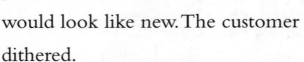

'I think he should look at it now,' said
Jack. 'It's got mud and dust on it.' He
meant, you can see it's the kind of car that
can take you on adventures.

The customer looked at Dad. Dad
shrugged and nodded. He pointed the way.

As they went, he looked back and winked at Jack.

'Looks like you might have sold another car for us!' he said.

Look out for more of Car-mad Jack's adventures in the following books:

The Speedy Sports Car
The Versatile Van
The Motorbike in the Mountains
The Marvellous Minibus
The Taxi about Town